_1_

By James Joyce

NORTH RICHMOND STREET, being blind, was quiet street except at the hour when the Christia Brothers' School set the boys free. An uninhabite house of two storeys stood at the blind enc detached from its neighbours in a square ground The other houses of the street, conscious of decen lives within them, gazed at one another with brow imperturbable faces.

The former tenant of our house, a priest, had die in the back drawing-room. Air, musty from havin; been long enclosed, hung in all the rooms, and th waste room behind the kitchen was littered with ol useless papers. Among these I found a few paper covered books, the pages of which were curled anc damp: *The Abbot*, by Walter Scott, *The Devou Communicant* and *The Memoirs of Vidocq*. I likec the last best because its leaves were yellow. The wild garden behind the house contained a centra apple-tree and a few straggling bushes under one o which I found the late tenant's rusty bicycle-pump He had been a very charitable priest; in his will h had left all his money to institutions and the furniture of his house to his sister.

When the short days of winter came dusk fell before we had well eaten our dinners. When we met in the street the houses had grown sombre. The space of sky above us was the colour of ever-changing violet and towards it the lamps of the street lifted their feeble lanterns. The cold air stung us and we played till our bodies glowed. Our shouts echoed in the silent street. The career of our play brought us through the dark muddy lanes behind the houses where we ran the gauntlet of the rough tribes from the cottages, to the back doors of the dark dripping gardens where odours arose from the ashpits, to the dark odorous stables where a coachman smoothed and combed the horse or shook music from the buckled harness. When we returned to the street light from the kitchen windows had filled the areas. If my uncle was seen turning the corner we hid in the shadow until we had seen him safely housed. Or if Mangan's sister came out on the doorstep to call her brother in to his tea we watched her from our shadow peer up and down the street. We waited to see whether she would remain or go in and, if she remained, we left our shadow and walked up to Mangan's steps resignedly. She was waiting for us, her figure defined by the light from the half-opened door. Her brother always teased her before he obeyed and I stood by the railings looking at her. Her dress swung as she moved her body and the soft rope of her hair tossed from side to side.

Every morning I lay on the floor in the front parlour watching her door. The blind was pulled down to within an inch of the sash so that I could not be seen. When she came out on the doorstep my heart leaped. I ran to the hall, seized my books and followed her. I kept her brown figure always in my eye and, when we came near the point at which our ways diverged, I quickened my pace and passed her. This happened morning after morning. I had never spoken to her, except for a few casual words, and yet her name was like a summons to all my foolish blood.

Her image accompanied me even in places the most hostile to romance. On Saturday evenings when my aunt went marketing I had to go to carry some of the parcels. We walked through the flaring streets, ostled by drunken men and bargaining women, mid the curses of labourers, the shrill litanies of hop-boys who stood on guard by the barrels of pigs' cheeks, the nasal chanting of street-singers, who sang a *come-all-you* about O'Donovan Rossa, or a ballad about the troubles in our native land. These noises converged in a single sensation of life for me: I imagined that I bore my chalice safely through a throng of foes. Her name sprang to my lips at moments in strange prayers and praises which I myself did not understand. My eyes were often full of tears (I could not tell why) and at times a flood from my heart seemed to pour itself out into my bosom. I thought little of the future. I did not know whether I would ever speak to her or not or, if I spoke to her, how I could tell her of my confused adoration. But my body was like a harp and her words and gestures were like fingers running upon the wires.

One evening I went into the back drawing-room in which the priest had died. It was a dark rainy evening and there was no sound in the house. Through one of the broken panes I heard the rain impinge upon the earth, the fine incessant needles of water playing in the sodden beds. Some distant lamp or lighted window gleamed below me. I was thankful that I could see so little. All my senses seemed to desire to veil themselves and, feeling that I was about to slip from them, I pressed the palms of my hands together until they trembled, murmuring: *"O love! O love!"* many times.

At last she spoke to me. When she addressed the first words to me I was so confused that I did not know what to answer. She asked me was I going to *Araby*. I forgot whether I answered yes or no. It would be a splendid bazaar, she said; she would love to go.

"And why can't you?" I asked.

While she spoke she turned a silver bracelet round and round her wrist. She could not go, she said, because there would be a retreat that week in her convent. Her brother and two other boys were fighting for their caps and I was alone at the railings. She held one of the spikes, bowing her head towards me. The light from the lamp opposite our door caught the white curve of her neck, lit up

er hair that rested there and, falling, lit up the hand
pon the railing. It fell over one side of her dress
nd caught the white border of a petticoat, just
isible as she stood at ease.

It's well for you," she said.

If I go," I said, "I will bring you something."

Vhat innumerable follies laid waste my waking
nd sleeping thoughts after that evening! I wished
) annihilate the tedious intervening days. I chafed
gainst the work of school. At night in my bedroom
nd by day in the classroom her image came
etween me and the page I strove to read. The
yllables of the word *Araby* were called to me
hrough the silence in which my soul luxuriated and
ast an Eastern enchantment over me. I asked for
eave to go to the bazaar on Saturday night. My
unt was surprised and hoped it was not some
reemason affair. I answered few questions in
lass. I watched my master's face pass from
miability to sternness; he hoped I was not
eginning to idle. I could not call my wandering
houghts together. I had hardly any patience with
he serious work of life which, now that it stood

between me and my desire, seemed to me child'
play, ugly monotonous child's play.

On Saturday morning I reminded my uncle that
wished to go to the bazaar in the evening. He wa
fussing at the hallstand, looking for the hat-brush
and answered me curtly:

"Yes, boy, I know."

As he was in the hall I could not go into the from
parlour and lie at the window. I left the house ir
bad humour and walked slowly towards the school
The air was pitilessly raw and already my hear
misgave me.

When I came home to dinner my uncle had not ye
been home. Still it was early. I sat staring at the
clock for some time and, when its ticking began to
irritate me, I left the room. I mounted the staircase
and gained the upper part of the house. The high
cold empty gloomy rooms liberated me and I wen
from room to room singing. From the front window
I saw my companions playing below in the street
Their cries reached me weakened and indistinc
and, leaning my forehead against the cool glass,
looked over at the dark house where she lived.

may have stood there for an hour, seeing nothing but the brown-clad figure cast by my imagination, touched discreetly by the lamplight at the curved neck, at the hand upon the railings and at the border below the dress.

When I came downstairs again I found Mrs Mercer sitting at the fire. She was an old garrulous woman, a pawnbroker's widow, who collected used stamps for some pious purpose. I had to endure the gossip of the tea-table. The meal was prolonged beyond an hour and still my uncle did not come. Mrs Mercer stood up to go: she was sorry she couldn't wait any longer, but it was after eight o'clock and she did not like to be out late as the night air was bad for her. When she had gone I began to walk up and down the room, clenching my fists. My aunt said: "I'm afraid you may put off your bazaar for this night of Our Lord."

At nine o'clock I heard my uncle's latchkey in the halldoor. I heard him talking to himself and heard the hallstand rocking when it had received the weight of his overcoat. I could interpret these signs. When he was midway through his dinner I asked him to give me the money to go to the bazaar. He had forgotten.

"The people are in bed and after their first sleep now," he said.

I did not smile. My aunt said to him energetically:

"Can't you give him the money and let him go? You've kept him late enough as it is."

My uncle said he was very sorry he had forgotten He said he believed in the old saying: "All work and no play makes Jack a dull boy." He asked me where I was going and, when I had told him a second time he asked me did I know *The Arab's Farewell to his Steed*. When I left the kitchen he was about to recite the opening lines of the piece to my aunt.

I held a florin tightly in my hand as I strode down Buckingham Street towards the station. The sight of the streets thronged with buyers and glaring with gas recalled to me the purpose of my journey. I took my seat in a third-class carriage of a deserted train. After an intolerable delay the train moved out of the station slowly. It crept onward among ruinous houses and over the twinkling river. At

Vestland Row Station a crowd of people pressed to the carriage doors; but the porters moved them back, saying that it was a special train for the bazaar. I remained alone in the bare carriage. In a few minutes the train drew up beside an improvised wooden platform. I passed out on to the road and saw by the lighted dial of a clock that it was ten minutes to ten. In front of me was a large building which displayed the magical name.

I could not find any sixpenny entrance and, fearing that the bazaar would be closed, I passed in quickly through a turnstile, handing a shilling to a weary-looking man. I found myself in a big hall girdled at half its height by a gallery. Nearly all the stall were closed and the greater part of the hall was i darkness. I recognised a silence like that which pervades a church after a service. I walked into the centre of the bazaar timidly. A few people wer gathered about the stalls which were still open Before a curtain, over which the words *Café Chantant* were written in coloured lamps, two men were counting money on a salver. I listened to the fall of the coins.

Remembering with difficulty why I had come went over to one of the stalls and examined porcelain vases and flowered tea-sets. At the doo of the stall a young lady was talking and laughing with two young gentlemen. I remarked thei English accents and listened vaguely to their conversation.

"O, I never said such a thing!"

"O, but you did!"

"O, but I didn't!"

"Didn't she say that?"

"Yes. I heard her."

"O, there's a ... fib!"

Observing me the young lady came over and asked me did I wish to buy anything. The tone of her voice was not encouraging; she seemed to have spoken to me out of a sense of duty. I looked humbly at the great jars that stood like eastern guards at either side of the dark entrance to the stall and murmured:

No, thank you."

The young lady changed the position of one of the vases and went back to the two young men. They began to talk of the same subject. Once or twice the young lady glanced at me over her shoulder.

I lingered before her stall, though I knew my stay was useless, to make my interest in her wares seem the more real. Then I turned away slowly and walked down the middle of the bazaar. I allowed the two pennies to fall against the sixpence in my pocket. I heard a voice call from one end of the gallery that the light was out. The upper part of the hall was now completely dark.

Gazing up into the darkness I saw myself as a creature driven and derided by vanity; and my eyes burned with anguish and anger.

EVELINE

SHE sat at the window watching the evening invade the avenue. Her head was leaned against the window curtains and in her nostrils was the odour of dusty cretonne. She was tired.

Few people passed. The man out of the last house passed on his way home; she heard his footsteps clacking along the concrete pavement and afterwards crunching on the cinder path before the new red houses. One time there used to be a field there in which they used to play every evening with other people's children. Then a man from Belfast bought the field and built houses in it—not like their little brown houses but bright brick houses with shining roofs. The children of the avenue used to play together in that field—the Devines, the Waters, the Dunns, little Keogh the cripple, she and her brothers and sisters. Ernest, however, never played: he was too grown up. Her father used often to hunt them in out of the field with his blackthorn stick; but usually little Keogh used to keep *nix* and call out when he saw her father coming. Still they seemed to have been rather happy then. Her father was not so bad then; and besides, her mother was alive. That was a long time ago; she and her brothers and sisters were all grown up; her mother was dead. Tizzie Dunn was dead, too, and the Waters had gone back to England. Everything changes. Now she was going to go away like the others, to leave her home.

Home! She looked round the room, reviewing all its familiar objects which she had dusted once a week for so many years, wondering where on earth all the dust came from. Perhaps she would never see again those familiar objects from which she had never dreamed of being divided. And yet during all those years she had never found out the name of the priest whose yellowing photograph hung on the wall above the broken harmonium beside the coloured print of the promises made to Blessed Margaret Mary Alacoque. He had been a school friend of her father. Whenever he showed the photograph to a visitor her father used to pass it with a casual word:

"He is in Melbourne now."

She had consented to go away, to leave her home. Was that wise? She tried to weigh each side of the question. In her home anyway she had shelter and food; she had those whom she had known all her life about her. Of course she had to work hard, both in the house and at business. What would they say of her in the Stores when they found out that she had run away with a fellow? Say she was a fool, erhaps; and her place would be filled up by dvertisement. Miss Gavan would be glad. She had lways had an edge on her, especially whenever here were people listening.

Miss Hill, don't you see these ladies are waiting?"

Look lively, Miss Hill, please."

She would not cry many tears at leaving the Stores.

But in her new home, in a distant unknown country, t would not be like that. Then she would be narried—she, Eveline. People would treat her with espect then. She would not be treated as her nother had been. Even now, though she was over nineteen, she sometimes felt herself in danger of her father's violence. She knew it was that that had given her the palpitations. When they were growing up he had never gone for her like he used to go for Harry and Ernest, because she was a girl; but latterly he had begun to threaten her and say what he would do to her only for her dead mother's sake. And now she had nobody to protect her. Ernest was dead and Harry, who was in the church decorating business, was nearly always down somewhere in the country. Besides, the invariable squabble for money on Saturday nights had begun to weary her unspeakably. She always gave her entire wages— seven shillings—and Harry always sent up what he could but the trouble was to get any money from her father. He said she used to squander the money, that she had no head, that he wasn't going to give her his hard-earned money to throw about the streets, and much more, for he was usually fairly bad of a Saturday night. In the end he would give her the money and ask her had she any intention of buying Sunday's dinner. Then she had to rush out as quickly as she could and do her marketing,

olding her black leather purse tightly in her hand
s she elbowed her way through the crowds and
eturning home late under her load of provisions.
he had hard work to keep the house together and
o see that the two young children who had been
eft to her charge went to school regularly and got
heir meals regularly. It was hard work—a hard life
—but now that she was about to leave it she did not
ind it a wholly undesirable life.

he was about to explore another life with Frank.
rank was very kind, manly, open-hearted. She was
o go away with him by the night-boat to be his
vife and to live with him in Buenos Ayres where he
ad a home waiting for her. How well she
emembered the first time she had seen him; he was
odging in a house on the main road where she used
o visit. It seemed a few weeks ago. He was
tanding at the gate, his peaked cap pushed back on
is head and his hair tumbled forward over a face
f bronze. Then they had come to know each other.
Ie used to meet her outside the Stores every
vening and see her home. He took her to see *The
Bohemian Girl* and she felt elated as she sat in an

unaccustomed part of the theatre with him. He wa
awfully fond of music and sang a little. Peopl
knew that they were courting and, when he san
about the lass that loves a sailor, she always fe
pleasantly confused. He used to call her Poppen
out of fun. First of all it had been an excitement fo
her to have a fellow and then she had begun to lik
him. He had tales of distant countries. He ha
started as a deck boy at a pound a month on a shi
of the Allan Line going out to Canada. He told he
the names of the ships he had been on and th
names of the different services. He had saile
through the Straits of Magellan and he told he
stories of the terrible Patagonians. He had fallen o
his feet in Buenos Ayres, he said, and had com
over to the old country just for a holiday. Of course
her father had found out the affair and ha
forbidden her to have anything to say to him.

"I know these sailor chaps," he said.

One day he had quarrelled with Frank and after tha
she had to meet her lover secretly.

The evening deepened in the avenue. The white o
two letters in her lap grew indistinct. One was t

Harry; the other was to her father. Ernest had been her favourite but she liked Harry too. Her father was becoming old lately, she noticed; he would miss her. Sometimes he could be very nice. Not long before, when she had been laid up for a day, he had read her out a ghost story and made toast for her at the fire. Another day, when their mother was alive, they had all gone for a picnic to the Hill of Howth. She remembered her father putting on her mother's bonnet to make the children laugh.

Her time was running out but she continued to sit by the window, leaning her head against the window curtain, inhaling the odour of dusty cretonne. Down far in the avenue she could hear a street organ playing. She knew the air. Strange that it should come that very night to remind her of the promise to her mother, her promise to keep the home together as long as she could. She remembered the last night of her mother's illness; she was again in the close dark room at the other side of the hall and outside she heard a melancholy air of Italy. The organ-player had been ordered to go away and given sixpence. She remembered her father strutting back into the sickroom saying: "Damned Italians! coming over here!"

As she mused the pitiful vision of her mother's life laid its spell on the very quick of her being—tha life of commonplace sacrifices closing in fina craziness. She trembled as she heard again her mother's voice saying constantly with foolish insistence:

"Derevaun Seraun! Derevaun Seraun!"

She stood up in a sudden impulse of terror. Escape! She must escape! Frank would save her. He would give her life, perhaps love, too. But she wanted to live. Why should she be unhappy? She had a right to happiness. Frank would take her in his arms, fold her in his arms. He would save her.

She stood among the swaying crowd in the station at the North Wall. He held her hand and she knew that he was speaking to her, saying something about the passage over and over again. The station was full of soldiers with brown baggages. Through the wide doors of the sheds she caught a glimpse of the black mass of the boat, lying in beside the quay wall, with illumined portholes. She answered nothing. She felt her cheek pale and cold and, out of a maze of distress, she prayed to God to direct her, to show her what was her duty. The boat blew a long mournful whistle into the mist. If she went, tomorrow she would be on the sea with Frank, steaming towards Buenos Ayres. Their passage had been booked. Could she still draw back after all he had done for her? Her distress awoke a nausea in her body and she kept moving her lips in silent fervent prayer.

A bell clanged upon her heart. She felt him seize her hand:

"Come!"

All the seas of the world tumbled about her heart. He was drawing her into them: he would drown her. She gripped with both hands at the iron railing.

"Come!"

No! No! No! It was impossible. Her hands clutched the iron in frenzy. Amid the seas she sent a cry of anguish!

"Eveline! Evvy!"

He rushed beyond the barrier and called to her to follow. He was shouted at to go on but he still called to her. She set her white face to him, passive like a helpless animal. Her eyes gave him no sign of love or farewell or recognition.

AFTER THE RACE

THE cars came scudding in towards Dublin running evenly like pellets in the groove of the Naas Road. At the crest of the hill at Inchicore sightseers had gathered in clumps to watch the cars careering homeward and through this channel of poverty and inaction the Continent sped its wealth and industry. Now and again the clumps of people raised the cheer of the gratefully oppressed. Their sympathy, however, was for the blue cars—the cars of their friends, the French.

he French, moreover, were virtual victors. Their
eam had finished solidly; they had been placed
econd and third and the driver of the winning
German car was reported a Belgian. Each blue car,
herefore, received a double measure of welcome as
t topped the crest of the hill and each cheer of
velcome was acknowledged with smiles and nods
by those in the car. In one of these trimly built cars
vas a party of four young men whose spirits
eemed to be at present well above the level of
uccessful Gallicism: in fact, these four young men

were almost hilarious. They were Charles Ségouin the owner of the car; André Rivière, a young electrician of Canadian birth; a huge Hungarian named Villona and a neatly groomed young man named Doyle. Ségouin was in good humour because he had unexpectedly received some orders in advance (he was about to start a motor establishment in Paris) and Rivière was in good humour because he was to be appointed manager of the establishment; these two young men (who were cousins) were also in good humour because of the success of the French cars. Villona was in good humour because he had had a very satisfactory luncheon; and besides he was an optimist by nature. The fourth member of the party, however, was too excited to be genuinely happy.

He was about twenty-six years of age, with a soft light brown moustache and rather innocent-looking grey eyes. His father, who had begun life as an advanced Nationalist, had modified his views early. He had made his money as a butcher in Kingstown and by opening shops in Dublin and in the suburbs he had made his money many times over. He had also been fortunate enough to secure some of the police contracts and in the end he had become rich enough to be alluded to in the Dublin newspapers as a merchant prince. He had sent his son to England to be educated in a big Catholic college and had afterwards sent him to Dublin University to study law. Jimmy did not study very earnestly and took to bad courses for a while. He had money and he was popular; and he divided his time curiously between musical and motoring circles. Then he had been sent for a term to Cambridge to see a little life. His father, remonstrative, but covertly proud of the excess, had paid his bills and brought him home. It was at Cambridge that he had met Ségouin. They were not much more than acquaintances as yet but Jimmy found great pleasure in the society of one who had seen so much of the world and was reputed to own some of the biggest hotels in France. Such a person (as his father agreed) was well worth knowing, even if he had not been the charming companion he was. Villona was entertaining also—a brilliant pianist—but, unfortunately, very poor.

The car ran on merrily with its cargo of hilarious youth. The two cousins sat on the front seat; Jimmy and his Hungarian friend sat behind. Decidedly Villona was in excellent spirits; he kept up a deep bass hum of melody for miles of the road. The Frenchmen flung their laughter and light words over their shoulders and often Jimmy had to strain forward to catch the quick phrase. This was not altogether pleasant for him, as he had nearly always to make a deft guess at the meaning and shout back a suitable answer in the face of a high wind. Besides Villona's humming would confuse anybody; the noise of the car, too.

Rapid motion through space elates one; so does notoriety; so does the possession of money. These were three good reasons for Jimmy's excitement. He had been seen by many of his friends that day in the company of these Continentals. At the control Ségouin had presented him to one of the French competitors and, in answer to his confused murmur of compliment, the swarthy face of the driver had disclosed a line of shining white teeth. It was pleasant after that honour to return to the profane world of spectators amid nudges and significant looks. Then as to money—he really had a great sum under his control. Ségouin, perhaps, would not think it a great sum but Jimmy who, in spite of temporary errors, was at heart the inheritor of solid instincts knew well with what difficulty it had been got together. This knowledge had previously kept his bills within the limits of reasonable recklessness, and, if he had been so conscious of the labour latent in money when there had been question merely of some freak of the higher intelligence, how much more so now when he was about to stake the greater part of his substance! It was a serious thing for him.

Of course, the investment was a good one and Ségouin had managed to give the impression that it was by a favour of friendship the mite of Irish money was to be included in the capital of the concern. Jimmy had a respect for his father's shrewdness in business matters and in this case it had been his father who had first suggested the investment; money to be made in the motor business, pots of money. Moreover Ségouin had the unmistakable air of wealth. Jimmy set out to translate into days' work that lordly car in which he sat. How smoothly it ran. In what style they had come careering along the country roads! The journey laid a magical finger on the genuine pulse of life and gallantly the machinery of human nerve strove to answer the bounding courses of the swift blue animal.

They drove down Dame Street. The street was busy with unusual traffic, loud with the horns of motorists and the gongs of impatient tram-drivers. Near the Bank Ségouin drew up and Jimmy and his friend alighted. A little knot of people collected on the footpath to pay homage to the snorting motor. The party was to dine together that evening in Ségouin's hotel and, meanwhile, Jimmy and his friend, who was staying with him, were to go home to dress. The car steered out slowly for Grafton Street while the two young men pushed their way through the knot of gazers. They walked northward with a curious feeling of disappointment in the exercise, while the city hung its pale globes of light above them in a haze of summer evening.

n Jimmy's house this dinner had been pronounced
n occasion. A certain pride mingled with his
arents' trepidation, a certain eagerness, also, to
lay fast and loose for the names of great foreign
ities have at least this virtue. Jimmy, too, looked
ery well when he was dressed and, as he stood in
ne hall giving a last equation to the bows of his
ress tie, his father may have felt even
ommercially satisfied at having secured for his son
ualities often unpurchaseable. His father,
nerefore, was unusually friendly with Villona and
is manner expressed a real respect for foreign
ccomplishments; but this subtlety of his host was
robably lost upon the Hungarian, who was
eginning to have a sharp desire for his dinner.

'he dinner was excellent, exquisite. Ségouin,
immy decided, had a very refined taste. The party
vas increased by a young Englishman named
Louth whom Jimmy had seen with Ségouin at
Cambridge. The young men supped in a snug room
it by electric candle-lamps. They talked volubly
nd with little reserve. Jimmy, whose imagination
vas kindling, conceived the lively youth of the

Frenchmen twined elegantly upon the firm framework of the Englishman's manner. A graceful image of his, he thought, and a just one. He admired the dexterity with which their host directed the conversation. The five young men had various tastes and their tongues had been loosened. Villona, with immense respect, began to discover to the mildly surprised Englishman the beauties of the English madrigal, deploring the loss of old instruments. Rivière, not wholly ingenuously, undertook to explain to Jimmy the triumph of the French mechanicians. The resonant voice of the

Hungarian was about to prevail in ridicule of the spurious lutes of the romantic painters when Ségouin shepherded his party into politics. Here was congenial ground for all. Jimmy, under generous influences, felt the buried zeal of his father wake to life within him: he aroused the torpid Routh at last. The room grew doubly hot and Ségouin's task grew harder each moment: there was even danger of personal spite. The alert host at an opportunity lifted his glass to Humanity and, when the toast had been drunk, he threw open a window significantly.

That night the city wore the mask of a capital. The five young men strolled along Stephen's Green in a faint cloud of aromatic smoke. They talked loudly and gaily and their cloaks dangled from their shoulders. The people made way for them. At the corner of Grafton Street a short fat man was putting two handsome ladies on a car in charge of another fat man. The car drove off and the short fat man caught sight of the party.

"André."

"It's Farley!"

A torrent of talk followed. Farley was an American. No one knew very well what the talk was about. Villona and Rivière were the noisiest, but all the men were excited. They got up on a car, squeezing themselves together amid much laughter. They drove by the crowd, blended now into soft colours, to a music of merry bells. They took the train at Westland Row and in a few seconds, as it seemed to Jimmy, they were walking out of Kingstown Station. The ticket-collector saluted Jimmy; he was an old man:

"Fine night, sir!"

It was a serene summer night; the harbour lay like a darkened mirror at their feet. They proceeded towards it with linked arms, singing *Cadet Roussel* in chorus, stamping their feet at every:

"Ho! Ho! Hohé, vraiment!"

They got into a rowboat at the slip and made out for the American's yacht. There was to be supper, music, cards. Villona said with conviction:

"It is delightful!"

There was a yacht piano in the cabin. Villona played a waltz for Farley and Rivière, Farley acting s cavalier and Rivière as lady. Then an impromptu quare dance, the men devising original figures. What merriment! Jimmy took his part with a will; his was seeing life, at least. Then Farley got out of breath and cried *"Stop!"* A man brought in a light upper, and the young men sat down to it for form's ake. They drank, however: it was Bohemian. They drank Ireland, England, France, Hungary, the United States of America. Jimmy made a speech, a long speech, Villona saying: *"Hear! Hear!"* whenever there was a pause. There was a great clapping of hands when he sat down. It must have been a good speech. Farley clapped him on the back and laughed loudly. What jovial fellows! What good company they were!

Cards! cards! The table was cleared. Villona returned quietly to his piano and played voluntaries for them. The other men played game after game, flinging themselves boldly into the adventure. They drank the health of the Queen of Hearts and of the Queen of Diamonds. Jimmy felt obscurely the lack of an audience: the wit was flashing. Play ran very high and paper began to pass. Jimmy did not know

exactly who was winning but he knew that he wa
losing. But it was his own fault for he frequentl
mistook his cards and the other men had to
calculate his I.O.U.'s for him. They were devils o
fellows but he wished they would stop: it wa
getting late. Someone gave the toast of th
yacht *The Belle of Newport* and then someon
proposed one great game for a finish.

The piano had stopped; Villona must have gone u
on deck. It was a terrible game. They stopped jus
before the end of it to drink for luck. Jimm
understood that the game lay between Routh anc
Ségouin. What excitement! Jimmy was excited too
he would lose, of course. How much had he writter
away? The men rose to their feet to play the las
tricks. talking and gesticulating. Routh won. Th
cabin shook with the young men's cheering and the
cards were bundled together. They began then tc
gather in what they had won. Farley and Jimmy
were the heaviest losers.

He knew that he would regret in the morning but a
present he was glad of the rest, glad of the darl
stupor that would cover up his folly. He leaned his

lbows on the table and rested his head between his ands, counting the beats of his temples. The cabin oor opened and he saw the Hungarian standing in shaft of grey light:

Daybreak, gentlemen!"

HERE IS A FREE BOOK

AS A BONUS GIFT

The Three Strangers

Thomas Hardy

About Hardy:

Thomas Hardy, OM (2 June 1840 – 11 January 1928) was an English novelist, short story writer, and poet of the naturalist movement. The bulk of his work, set mainly in the semi-imaginary county of Wessex, delineates characters struggling against their passions and circumstances. Hardy's poetry, first published in his fifties, has come to be as well regarded as his novels, especially after the 1960s Movement.

AMONG the few features of agricultural England which retain an appearance but little modified by the lapse of centuries, may be reckoned the high, grassy and furzy downs, coombs, or ewe-leases, as they are indifferently called, that fill a large area of certain counties in the south and south-west. If any mark of human occupation is met with hereon, it usually takes the form of the solitary cottage of some shepherd.

Fifty years ago such a lonely cottage stood on such a down, and may possibly be standing there now. In spite of its loneliness, however, the spot, by actual measurement, was not more than five miles from a county-town. Yet that affected it little. Five miles of irregular upland, during the long inimical seasons, with their sleets, snows, rains, and mists, afford withdrawing space enough to isolate a Timon or a Nebuchadnezzar; much less, in fair weather, to please that less repellent tribe, the poets, philosophers, artists, and others who 'conceive and meditate of pleasant things.'

Some old earthen camp or barrow, some clump of trees, at least some starved fragment of ancient hedge is usually taken advantage of in the erection of these forlorn dwellings. But, in the present case such a kind of shelter had been disregarded. Highe Crowstairs, as the house was called, stood quit detached and undefended. The only reason for it precise situation seemed to be the crossing of two footpaths at right angles hard by, which may hav crossed there and thus for a good five hundred years. Hence the house was exposed to the elements on all sides. But, though the wind up her blew unmistakably when it did blow, and the rain hit hard whenever it fell, the various weathers o the winter season were not quite so formidable or the coomb as they were imagined to be by dweller: on low ground. The raw rimes were not so pernicious as in the hollows, and the frosts were scarcely so severe. When the shepherd and hi family who tenanted the house were pitied for thei sufferings from the exposure, they said that upor the whole they were less inconvenienced by 'wuzzes and flames' (hoarses and phlegms) thar when they had lived by the stream of a snug neighbouring valley.

he night of March 28, 182-, was precisely one of ae nights that were wont to call forth these xpressions of commiseration. The level rainstorm note walls, slopes, and hedges like the clothyard ꞁafts of Senlac and Crecy. Such sheep and outdoor nimals as had no shelter stood with their buttocks ꞁ the winds; while the tails of little birds trying to ꞁost on some scraggy thorn were blown inside-out ke umbrellas. The gable-end of the cottage was tained with wet, and the eavesdroppings flapped gainst the wall. Yet never was commiseration for ꞁe shepherd more misplaced. For that cheerful ustic was entertaining a large party in glorification f the christening of his second girl.

ꞁhe guests had arrived before the rain began to fall, nd they were all now assembled in the chief or ꞁving room of the dwelling. A glance into the partment at eight o'clock on this eventful evening ꞁould have resulted in the opinion that it was as osy and comfortable a nook as could be wished for ꞁ boisterous weather. The calling of its inhabitant ꞁas proclaimed by a number of highly-polished heep-crooks without stems that were hung

ornamentally over the fireplace, the curl of eac
shining crook varying from the antiquated typ
engraved in the patriarchal pictures of old famil
Bibles to the most approved fashion of the last loca
sheep-fair. The room was lighted by half-a-doze
candles, having wicks only a trifle smaller than th
grease which enveloped them, in candlesticks tha
were never used but at high-days, holy-days, an
family feasts. The lights were scattered about th
room, two of them standing on the chimney-piece
This position of candles was in itself significant
Candles on the chimney-piece always meant
party.

On the hearth, in front of a back-brand to giv
substance, blazed a fire of thorns, that crackled 'lik
the laughter of the fool.'

Nineteen persons were gathered here. Of these, fiv
women, wearing gowns of various bright hues, sa
in chairs along the wall; girls shy and not shy fille
the window-bench; four men, including Charle
Jake the hedge-carpenter, Elijah New the parish
clerk, and John Pitcher, a neighbouring dairyman
the shepherd's father-in-law, lolled in the settle; a

young man and maid, who were blushing over tentative pourparlers on a life-companionship, sat beneath the corner-cupboard; and an elderly engaged man of fifty or upward moved restlessly about from spots where his betrothed was not to the spot where she was. Enjoyment was pretty general, and so much the more prevailed in being unhampered by conventional restrictions. Absolute confidence in each other's good opinion begat perfect ease, while the finishing stroke of manner, amounting to a truly princely serenity, was lent to the majority by the absence of any expression or trait denoting that they wished to get on in the world, enlarge their minds, or do any eclipsing thing whatever—which nowadays so generally nips the bloom and bonhomie of all except the two extremes of the social scale.

Shepherd Fennel had married well, his wife being a dairyman's daughter from a vale at a distance, who brought fifty guineas in her pocket—and kept them there, till they should be required for ministering to the needs of a coming family. This frugal woman had been somewhat exercised as to the character that should be given to the gathering. A sit-still party had its advantages; but an undisturbed position of ease in chairs and settles was apt to lead on the men to such an unconscionable deal of toping that they would sometimes fairly drink the ouse dry. A dancing-party was the alternative; but his, while avoiding the foregoing objection on the core of good drink, had a counterbalancing lisadvantage in the matter of good victuals, the avenous appetites engendered by the exercise ausing immense havoc in the buttery. Shepherdess 'ennel fell back upon the intermediate plan of ningling short dances with short periods of talk nd singing, so as to hinder any ungovernable rage n either. But this scheme was entirely confined to ler own gentle mind: the shepherd himself was in he mood to exhibit the most reckless phases of ospitality.

The fiddler was a boy of those parts, about twelve years of age, who had a wonderful dexterity in jigs nd reels, though his fingers were so small and hort as to necessitate a constant shifting for the ligh notes, from which he scrambled back to the irst position with sounds not of unmixed purity of one. At seven the shrill tweedle-dee of this youngster had begun, accompanied by a booming ground-bass from Elijah New, the parish-clerk, who lad thoughtfully brought with him his favourite musical instrument, the serpent. Dancing wa instantaneous, Mrs. Fennel privately enjoining th players on no account to let the dance exceed th length of a quarter of an hour.

But Elijah and the boy, in the excitement of thei position, quite forgot the injunction. Moreovei Oliver Giles, a man of seventeen, one of th dancers, who was enamoured of his partner, a fai girl of thirty-three rolling years, had recklessl handed a new crown-piece to the musicians, as bribe to keep going as long as they had muscle anc wind. Mrs. Fennel, seeing the steam begin tc generate on the countenances of her guests, crossec over and touched the fiddler's elbow and put he hand on the serpent's mouth. But they took nc notice, and fearing she might lose her character o genial hostess if she were to interfere too markedly she retired and sat down helpless. And so the danc whizzed on with cumulative fury, the performer: moving in their planet-like courses, direct anc retrograde, from apogee to perigee, till the hand o the well-kicked clock at the bottom of the room hac travelled over the circumference of an hour.

While these cheerful events were in course of enactment within Fennel's pastoral dwelling, an incident having considerable bearing on the party had occurred in the gloomy night without. Mrs. Fennel's concern about the growing fierceness of the dance corresponded in point of time with the ascent of a human figure to the solitary hill of Higher Crowstairs from the direction of the distant town. This personage strode on through the rain without a pause, following the little-worn path which, further on in its course, skirted the shepherd's cottage.

It was nearly the time of full moon, and on this account, though the sky was lined with a uniform sheet of dripping cloud, ordinary objects out of doors were readily visible. The sad wan light revealed the lonely pedestrian to be a man of supple frame; his gait suggested that he had somewhat passed the period of perfect and instinctive agility, though not so far as to be otherwise than rapid of motion when occasion required. At a rough guess, he might have been about forty years of age. He appeared tall, but a recruiting sergeant, or other person accustomed to the judging of men's height by the eye, would have discerned that this wa chiefly owing to his gauntness, and that he was no more than five-feet-eight or nine.

Notwithstanding the regularity of his tread, ther was caution in it, as in that of one who mentall feels his way; and despite the fact that it was not black coat nor a dark garment of any sort that h wore, there was something about him whic suggested that he naturally belonged to the black coated tribes of men. His clothes were of fustial and his boots hobnailed, yet in his progress h showed not the mud-accustomed bearing c hobnailed and fustianed peasantry.

By the time that he had arrived abreast of th shepherd's premises the rain came down, or rathe came along, with yet more determined violence The outskirts of the little settlement partially brok the force of wind and rain, and this induced him t stand still. The most salient of the shepherd' domestic erections was an empty sty at the forwar corner of his hedgeless garden, for in these latitude the principle of masking the homelier features o your establishment by a conventional frontage was unknown. The traveller's eye was attracted to this small building by the pallid shine of the wet slates that covered it. He turned aside, and, finding it empty, stood under the pent-roof for shelter.

While he stood, the boom of the serpent within the adjacent house, and the lesser strains of the fiddler, reached the spot as an accompaniment to the surging hiss of the flying rain on the sod, its louder beating on the cabbage-leaves of the garden, on the eight or ten beehives just discernible by the path, and its dripping from the eaves into a row of buckets and pans that had been placed under the walls of the cottage. For at Higher Crowstairs, as at all such elevated domiciles, the grand difficulty of housekeeping was an insufficiency of water; and a casual rainfall was utilized by turning out, as catchers, every utensil that the house contained. Some queer stories might be told of the contrivances for economy in suds and dish-waters that are absolutely necessitated in upland habitations during the droughts of summer. But at this season there were no such exigencies; a mere acceptance of what the skies bestowed was sufficient for an abundant store.

At last the notes of the serpent ceased and the house was silent. This cessation of activity aroused the solitary pedestrian from the reverie into which he had lapsed, and, emerging from the shed, with an apparently new intention, he walked up the path to the house-door. Arrived here, his first act was to kneel down on a large stone beside the row of vessels, and to drink a copious draught from one of them. Having quenched his thirst he rose and lifted his hand to knock, but paused with his eye upon the panel. Since the dark surface of the wood revealed absolutely nothing, it was evident that he must be mentally looking through the door, as if he wished to measure thereby all the possibilities that a house of this sort might include, and how they might bear upon the question of his entry.

In his indecision he turned and surveyed the scene around. Not a soul was anywhere visible. The garden-path stretched downward from his feet, gleaming like the track of a snail the roof of the little well (mostly dry), the well-cover, the top rail f the garden-gate, were varnished with the same dull liquid glaze; while, far away in the vale, a faint whiteness of more than usual extent showed that the rivers were high in the meads. Beyond all this winked a few bleared lamplights through the beating drops—lights that denoted the situation of the county-town from which he had appeared to come. The absence of all notes of life in that direction seemed to clinch his intentions, and he knocked at the door.

Within, a desultory chat had taken the place of movement and musical sound. The hedge-carpenter was suggesting a song to the company, which nobody just then was inclined to undertake, so that the knock afforded a not unwelcome diversion.

Walk in!' said the shepherd promptly.

The latch clicked upward, and out of the night ou
pedestrian appeared upon the door-mat. The
shepherd arose, snuffed two of the nearest candles
and turned to look at him.

Their light disclosed that the stranger was dark ir
complexion and not unprepossessing as to feature
His hat, which for a moment he did not remove
hung low over his eyes, without concealing tha
they were large, open, and determined, moving
with a flash rather than a glance round the room
He seemed pleased with his survey, and, baring his

haggy head, said, in a rich deep voice, 'The rain is
so heavy, friends, that I ask leave to come in and
rest awhile.'

'To be sure, stranger,' said the shepherd. 'And faith,
you've been lucky in choosing your time, for we are
having a bit of a fling for a glad cause—though, to
be sure, a man could hardly wish that glad cause to
happen more than once a year.'

'Nor less,' spoke up a woman. 'For 'tis best to get
your family over and done with, as soon as you
can, so as to be all the earlier out of the fag o't.'

'And what may be this glad cause?' asked the
stranger.

'A birth and christening,' said the shepherd.

The stranger hoped his host might not be made
unhappy either by too many or too few of such
episodes, and being invited by a gesture to a pull at
the mug, he readily acquiesced. His manner, which,
before entering, had been so dubious, was now
altogether that of a careless and candid man.

'Late to be traipsing athwart this coomb—hey?' said
the engaged man of fifty.

'Late it is, master, as you say.—I'll take a seat in the

chimney-corner, if you have nothing to urge again:
it, ma'am; for I am a little moist on the side tha
was next the rain.'

Mrs. Shepherd Fennel assented, and made room fc
the self-invited comer, who, having got completel
inside the chimney-corner, stretched out his leg
and his arms with the expansiveness of a perso
quite at home.

'Yes, I am rather cracked in the vamp,' he sai
freely, seeing that the eyes of the shepherd's wif
fell upon his boots, 'and I am not well fitted either.
have had some rough times lately, and have bee
forced to pick up what I can get in the way o
wearing, but I must find a suit better fit fo
working-days when I reach home.'

'One of hereabouts?' she inquired.

'Not quite that—further up the country.'

'I thought so. And so be I; and by your tongue yo
come from my neighbourhood.'

'But you would hardly have heard of me,' he sai
quickly. 'My time would be long before yours
ma'am, you see.'

This testimony to the youthfulness of his hostes

had the effect of stopping her cross-examination.
'There is only one thing more wanted to make me
happy,' continued the new-comer. 'And that is a
little baccy, which I am sorry to say I am out of.'
'I'll fill your pipe,' said the shepherd.
'I must ask you to lend me a pipe likewise.'
'A smoker, and no pipe about 'ee?'
'I have dropped it somewhere on the road.'
The shepherd filled and handed him a new clay
pipe, saying, as he did so, 'Hand me your baccy-
box—I'll fill that too, now I am about it.'
The man went through the movement of searching
his pockets.
'Lost that too? ' said his entertainer, with some
surprise.
'I am afraid so,' said the man with some confusion.
'Give it to me in a screw of paper.' Lighting his pipe
at the candle with a suction that drew the whole
flame into the bowl, he resettled himself in the
corner and bent his looks upon the faint steam from
his damp legs, as if he wished to say no more.
Meanwhile the general body of guests had been
taking little notice of this visitor by reason of an

absorbing discussion in which they were engaged with the band about a tune for the next dance. The matter being settled, they were about to stand up when an interruption came in the shape of another knock at the door.

At sound of the same the man in the chimney-corner took up the poker and began stirring the brands as if doing it thoroughly were the one aim of his existence; and a second time the shepherd said 'Walk in!' In a moment another man stood upon the straw-woven door-mat. He too was a stranger.

This individual was one of a type radically different from the first. There was more of the commonplace in his manner, and a certain jovial cosmopolitanism sat upon his features. He was several years older than the first arrival, his hair being slightly frosted, his eyebrows bristly, and his whiskers cut back from his cheeks. His face was rather full and flabby, and yet it was not altogether a face without power. A few grog-blossoms marked the neighbourhood of his nose. He flung back his long drab greatcoat, revealing that beneath it he wore a suit of cinder-gray shade throughout, large heavy eals, of some metal or other that would take a polish, dangling from his fob as his only personal ornament. Shaking the water-drops from his low-crowned glazed hat, he said, 'I must ask for a few minutes' shelter, comrades, or I shall be wetted to my skin before I get to Casterbridge.'

'Make yourself at home, master,' said the shepherd, perhaps a trifle less heartily than on the first occasion. Not that Fennel had the least tinge of niggardliness in his composition; but the room was far from large, spare chairs were not numerous, and damp companions were not altogether desirable at close quarters for the women and girls in their bright-coloured gowns.

However, the second comer, after taking off his greatcoat, and hanging his hat on a nail in one of the ceiling-beams as if he had been specially invited to put it there, advanced and sat down at the table. This had been pushed so closely into the chimney-corner, to give all available room to the dancers, that its inner edge grazed the elbow of the man who had ensconced himself by the fire; and thus the two strangers were brought into close

companionship. They nodded to each other by way of breaking the ice of unacquaintance, and the first stranger handed his neighbour the family mug—a huge vessel of brown ware, having its upper edge worn away like a threshold by the rub of whole generations of thirsty lips that had gone the way of all flesh, and bearing the following inscription burnt upon its rotund side in yellow letters:—
THERE IS NO FUN UNTILL i CUM.
The other man, nothing loth, raised the mug to his lips, and drank on, and on, and on—till a curiou

lueness overspread the countenance of the shepherd's wife, who had regarded with no little surprise the first stranger's free offer to the second of what did not belong to him to dispense.

knew it!' said the toper to the shepherd with much satisfaction. 'When I walked up your garden before coming in, and saw the hives all of a row, I said to myself, "Where there's bees there's honey, and where there's honey there's mead." But mead of such a truly comfortable sort as this I really didn't expect to meet in my older days.' He took yet another pull at the mug, till it assumed an ominous elevation.

'Glad you enjoy it!' I said the shepherd warmly.

't is goodish mead,' assented Mrs. Fennel, with an absence of enthusiasm which seemed to say that it was possible to buy praise for one's cellar at too heavy a price. 'It is trouble enough to make—and really I hardly think we shall make any more. For honey sells well, and we ourselves can make shift with a drop o' small mead and metheglin for common use from the comb-washings.'

'O, but you'll never have the heart!' reproachfully

cried the stranger in cinder-gray, after taking up the mug a third time and setting it down empty. 'I love mead, when 'tis old like this, as I love to go to church o' Sundays, or to relieve the needy any day of the week.'

'Ha, ha, ha!' said the man in the chimney-corner who, in spite of the taciturnity induced by the pipe of tobacco, could not or would not refrain from this slight testimony to his comrade's humour.

Now the old mead of those days, brewed of the purest first-year or maiden honey, four pounds to the gallon—with its due complement of white of eggs, cinnamon, ginger, cloves, mace, rosemary, yeast, and processes of working, bottling, and cellaring—tasted remarkably strong; but it did not taste so strong as it actually was. Hence, presently, the stranger in cinder-gray at the table, moved by its creeping influence, unbuttoned his waistcoat, threw himself back in his chair, spread his legs, and made his presence felt in various ways.

'Well, well, as I say,' he resumed, 'I am going to Casterbridge, and to Casterbridge I must go. should have been almost there by this time; but the

ain drove me into your dwelling, and I'm not sorry
or it.'

You don't live in Casterbridge?' said the shepherd.

Not as yet; though I shortly mean to move there.'

Going to set up in trade, perhaps?'

No, no,' said the shepherd's wife. 'It is easy to see
hat the gentleman is rich, and don't want to work at
anything.'

The cinder-gray stranger paused, as if to consider
whether he would accept that definition of himself.
He presently rejected it by answering, 'Rich is not
quite the word for me, dame. I do work, and I must
work. And even if I only get to Casterbridge by
midnight I must begin work there at eight to-
morrow morning. Yes, het or wet, blow or snow,
famine or sword, my day's work to-morrow must
be done.'

'Poor man! Then, in spite o' seeming, you be worse
off than we?' replied the shepherd's wife.

Tis the nature of my trade, men and maidens. 'Tis
the nature of my trade more than my poverty… .
But really and truly I must up and off, or I shan't
get a lodging in the town.' However, the speaker

did not move, and directly added, 'There's time fo
one more draught of friendship before I go; and I'c
perform it at once if the mug were not dry.'

'Here's a mug o' small,' said Mrs. Fennel. 'Small
we call it, though to be sure 'tis only the first wasl
o' the combs.'

'No,' said the stranger disdainfully. 'I won't spoi
your first kindness by partaking o' your second.'

'Certainly not,' broke in Fennel. 'We don't increase
and multiply every day, and I'll fill the mug again.
He went away to the dark place under the stairs
where the barrel stood. The shepherdess followec
him.

'Why should you do this? ' she said reproachfully
as soon as they were alone. 'He's emptied it once
though it held enough for ten people; and now he's
not contented wi' the small, but must needs call fo⟩
more o' the strong! And a stranger unbeknown tc
any of us. For my part, I don't like the look o' the
man at all.'

'But he's in the house, my honey; and 'tis a wet
night, and a christening. Daze it, what's a cup o⟩
mead more or less? There'll be plenty more nex⟩

ee-burning.'

'Very well—this time, then,' she answered, looking wistfully at the barrel. 'But what is the man's calling, and where is he one of, that he should come in and join us like this?'

'I don't know. I'll ask him again.'

The catastrophe of having the mug drained dry at one pull by the stranger in cinder-gray was effectually guarded against this time by Mrs. Fennel. She poured out his allowance in a small cup, keeping the large one at a discreet distance from him. When he had tossed off his portion the shepherd renewed his inquiry about the stranger's occupation.

The latter did not immediately reply, and the man in the chimney-corner, with sudden demonstrativeness, said, 'Anybody may know my trade—I'm a wheel-wright.'

'A very good trade for these parts,' said the shepherd.

'And anybody may know mine—if they've the sense to find it out,' said the stranger in cinder-gray.

'You may generally tell what a man is by his claws,'

observed the hedge-carpenter, looking at his own hands. 'My fingers be as full of thorns as an old pin-cushion is of pins.'

The hands of the man in the chimney-corner instinctively sought the shade, and he gazed into the fire as he resumed his pipe. The man at the table took up the hedge-carpenter's remark, and added smartly, 'True; but the oddity of my trade is that, instead of setting a mark upon me, it sets a mark upon my customers.'

No observation being offered by anybody in elucidation of this enigma, the shepherd's wife once more called for a song. The same obstacles presented themselves as at the former time—one had no voice, another had forgotten the first verse. The stranger at the table, whose soul had now risen to a good working temperature, relieved the difficulty by exclaiming that, to start the company, he would sing himself. Thrusting one thumb into the arm-hole of his waistcoat, he waved the other hand in the air, and, with an extemporizing gaze at the shining sheep-crooks above the mantelpiece, began:—

) my trade it is the rarest one, Simple shepherds ll— My trade is a sight to see; For my customers I e, and take them up on high, And waft 'em to a far untree!'

he room was silent when he had finished the verse —with one exception, that of the man in the himney-corner, who, at the singer's word, Chorus!' joined him in a deep bass voice of usical relish—

And waft 'em to a far countree!'

liver Giles, John Pitcher the dairyman, the parish-lerk, the engaged man of fifty, the row of young omen against the wall, seemed lost in thought not f the gayest kind. The shepherd looked neditatively on the ground, the shepherdess gazed eenly at the singer, and with some suspicion; she vas doubting whether this stranger were merely inging an old song from recollection, or was omposing one there and then for the occasion. All vere as perplexed at the obscure revelation as the uests at Belshazzar's Feast, except the man in the himney-corner, who quietly said, 'Second verse, tranger,' and smoked on.

The singer thoroughly moistened himself from his lips inwards, and went on with the next stanza as requested:—

'My tools are but common ones, Simple shepherd all— My tools are no sight to see: A little hempen string, and a post whereon to swing Are implements enough for me!'

Shepherd Fennel glanced round. There was no longer any doubt that the stranger was answering his question rhythmically. The guests one and all started back with suppressed exclamations. The young woman engaged to the man of fifty fainted half-way, and would have proceeded, but finding him wanting in alacrity for catching her she sat down trembling.

O, he's the ——!' whispered the people in the background, mentioning the name of an ominous public officer. 'He's come to do it! 'Tis to be at Casterbridge jail to-morrow—the man for sheep-stealing—the poor clock-maker we heard of, who used to live away at Shottsford and had no work to do—Timothy Summers, whose family were a-starving, and so he went out of Shottsford by the high-road, and took a sheep in open daylight, defying the farmer and the farmer's wife and the farmer's lad, and every man jack among 'em. He' (and they nodded towards the stranger of the deadly trade) 'is come from up the country to do it because there's not enough to do in his own county-town, and he's got the place here now our own county man's dead; he's going to live in the same cottage under the prison wall.'

The stranger in cinder-gray took no notice of this whispered string of observations, but again wetted his lips. Seeing that his friend in the chimney corner was the only one who reciprocated his joviality in any way, he held out his cup towards that appreciative comrade, who also held out his own. They clinked together, the eyes of the rest of the room hanging upon the singer's actions. He parted his lips for the third verse; but at that moment another knock was audible upon the door. This time the knock was faint and hesitating.

The company seemed scared; the shepherd looked with consternation towards the entrance, and it was with some effort that he resisted his alarmed wife's deprecatory glance, and uttered for the third time the welcoming words, 'Walk in!'

The door was gently opened, and another man stood upon the mat. He, like those who had preceded him, was a stranger. This time it was a short, small personage, of fair complexion, and dressed in a decent suit of dark clothes.

'Can you tell me the way to——?' he began: when, gazing round the room to observe the nature of the company amongst whom he had fallen, his eyes lighted on the stranger in cinder-gray. It was just at he instant when the latter, who had thrown his mind into his song with such a will that he scarcely needed the interruption, silenced all whispers and inquiries by bursting into his third verse:—

'To-morrow is my working day, Simple shepherds all— To-morrow is a working day for me: For the farmer's sheep is slain, and the lad who did it ta'en, And on his soul may God ha' merc-y!'

The stranger in the chimney-corner, waving cups with the singer so heartily that his mead splashed over on the hearth, repeated in his bass voice as before:—

'And on his soul may God ha' merc-y!'

All this time the third stranger had been standing in the doorway. Finding now that he did not come forward or go on speaking, the guests particularly regarded him. They noticed to their surprise that he stood before them the picture of abject terror—his knees trembling, his hand shaking so violently that the door-latch by which he supported himself rattled audibly: his white lips were parted, and his eyes fixed on the merry officer of justice in the middle of the room. A moment more and he had turned, closed the door, and fled.

'What a man can it be?' said the shepherd.

The rest, between the awfulness of their late discovery and the odd conduct of this third visitor, looked as if they knew not what to think, and said nothing. Instinctively they withdrew further and further from the grim gentleman in their midst, whom some of them seemed to take for the Prince of Darkness himself, till they formed a remote circle, an empty space of floor being left between them and him—

'… circulus, cujus centrum diabolus.'

The room was so silent—though there were more than twenty people in it—that nothing could be heard but the patter of the rain against the window-shutters, accompanied by the occasional hiss of a stray drop that fell down the chimney into the fire, and the steady puffing of the man in the corner who had now resumed his pipe of long clay.

The stillness was unexpectedly broken. The distant sound of a gun reverberated through the air— apparently from the direction of the county-town.

'Be jiggered!' cried the stranger who had sung the

ong, jumping up.

'What does that mean?' asked several.

'A prisoner has escaped from the jail—that's what means.'

All listened. The sound was repeated, and none of them spoke but the man in the chimney-corner, who said quietly, 'I've often been told that in this county they fire a gun at such times; but I never heard it till now.'

'I wonder if it is my man?' murmured the personage in cinder-gray.

'Surely it is!' said the shepherd involuntarily. 'And surely we've zeed him! That little man who looked in at the door by now, and quivered like a leaf when he zeed ye and heard your song!'

'His teeth chattered, and the breath went out of his body,' said the dairyman.

'And his heart seemed to sink within him like a stone,' said Oliver Giles.

'And he bolted as if he'd been shot at,' said the hedge-carpenter.

'True—his teeth chattered, and his heart seemed to sink; and he bolted as if he'd been shot at,' slowly summed up the man in the chimney-corner.

'I didn't notice it,' remarked the hangman.

'We were all a-wondering what made him run off i
such a fright,' faltered one of the women against th
wall, 'and now 'tis explained!'

The firing of the alarm-gun went on at interval.
low and sullenly, and their suspicions became
certainty. The sinister gentleman in cinder-gra
roused himself. 'Is there a constable here?' h
asked, in thick tones. 'If so, let him step forward.'

The engaged man of fifty stepped quavering ou
from the wall, his betrothed beginning to sob on th
back of the chair.

You are a sworn constable?'

I be, sir.'

Then, pursue the criminal at once, with assistance, and bring him back here. He can't have gone far.'

I will sir, I will—when I've got my staff. I'll go home and get it, and come sharp here, and start in a body.'

Staff!—never mind your staff; the man'll be gone!'

But I can't do nothing without my staff—can I, William, and John, and Charles Jake? No; for there's the king's royal crown a painted on en in yaller and gold, and the lion and the unicorn, so as when I raise en up and hit my prisoner, 'tis made a lawful blow thereby. I wouldn't 'tempt to take up a man without my staff—no, not I. If I hadn't the law to gie me courage, why, instead o' my taking up him he might take up me!'

Now, I'm a king's man myself, and can give you authority enough for this,' said the formidable officer in gray. 'Now then, all of ye, be ready. Have ye any lanterns?'

'Yes—have ye any lanterns?—I demand it!' said the constable.

'And the rest of you able-bodied——'

'Able-bodied men—yes—the rest of ye!' said the constable.

'Have you some good stout staves and pitch-forks——'

'Staves and pitchforks—in the name o' the law! And take 'em in yer hands and go in quest, and do as we in authority tell ye!'

Thus aroused, the men prepared to give chase. The evidence was, indeed, though circumstantial, so convincing, that but little argument was needed to show the shepherd's guests that after what they had seen it would look very much like connivance if they did not instantly pursue the unhappy third stranger, who could not as yet have gone more than a few hundred yards over such uneven country.

A shepherd is always well provided with lanterns and, lighting these hastily, and with hurdle-staves in their hands, they poured out of the door, taking a direction along the crest of the hill, away from the town, the rain having fortunately a little abated.

Disturbed by the noise, or possibly by unpleasant dreams of her baptism, the child who had been hristened began to cry heart-brokenly in the room verhead. These notes of grief came down through he chinks of the floor to the ears of the women elow, who jumped up one by one, and seemed lad of the excuse to ascend and comfort the baby, or the incidents of the last half-hour greatly ppressed them. Thus in the space of two or three ninutes the room on the ground-floor was deserted uite.

But it was not for long. Hardly had the sound of ootsteps died away when a man returned round the orner of the house from the direction the pursuers ad taken. Peeping in at the door, and seeing obody there, he entered leisurely. It was the tranger of the chimney-corner, who had gone out vith the rest. The motive of his return was shown y his helping himself to a cut piece of skimmer-ake that lay on a ledge beside where he had sat, nd which he had apparently forgotten to take with iim. He also poured out half a cup more mead from he quantity that remained, ravenously eating and lrinking these as he stood. He had not finished vhen another figure came in just as quietly—his friend in cinder-gray.

'O—you here?' said the latter, smiling. 'I though you had gone to help in the capture.' And thi speaker also revealed the object of his return b looking solicitously round for the fascinating mu; of old mead.

'And I thought you had gone,' said the other continuing his skimmer-cake with some effort.

'Well, on second thoughts, I felt there were enoug without me,' said the first confidentially, 'and such : night as it is, too. Besides, 'tis the business o' the Government to take care of its criminals—no mine.'

'True; so it is. And I felt as you did, that there were enough without me.'

'I don't want to break my limbs running over the humps and hollows of this wild country.'

'Nor I neither, between you and me.'

'These shepherd-people are used to it—simple minded souls, you know, stirred up to anything in a moment. They'll have him ready for me before the morning, and no trouble to me at all.'

'They'll have him, and we shall have savec

urselves all labour in the matter.'

'rue, true. Well, my way is to Casterbridge; and 'tis
s much as my legs will do to take me that far.
oing the same way?'

No, I am sorry to say! I have to get home over
iere' (he nodded indefinitely to the right), 'and I
eel as you do, that it is quite enough for my legs to
o before bedtime.'

'he other had by this time finished the mead in the
iug, after which, shaking hands heartily at the
oor, and wishing each other well, they went their
everal ways.

1 the meantime the company of pursuers had
eached the end of the hog's-back elevation which
ominated this part of the down. They had decided
n no particular plan of action; and, finding that the
ian of the baleful trade was no longer in their
ompany, they seemed quite unable to form any
uch plan now. They descended in all directions
own the hill, and straightway several of the party
ell into the snare set by Nature for all misguided
iidnight ramblers over this part of the cretaceous
ormation. The 'lanchets,' or flint slopes, which

belted the escarpment at intervals of a dozen yard
took the less cautious ones unawares, and losin
their footing on the rubbly steep they slid sharpl
downwards, the lanterns rolling from their hands t
the bottom, and there lying on their sides till th
horn was scorched through.

When they had again gathered themselves togethe
the shepherd, as the man who knew the countr
best, took the lead, and guided them round thes
treacherous inclines. The lanterns, which seeme
rather to dazzle their eyes and warn the fugitiv
than to assist them in the exploration, wer
extinguished, due silence was observed; and in thi
more rational order they plunged into the vale. I
was a grassy, briery, moist defile, affording som
shelter to any person who had sought it; but th
party perambulated it in vain, and ascended on th
other side. Here they wandered apart, and after a
interval closed together again to report progress. A
the second time of closing in they found themselve
near a lonely ash, the single tree on this part of th
coomb, probably sown there by a passing bird som
fifty years before. And here, standing a little to on

side of the trunk, as motionless as the trunk itself, appeared the man they were in quest of, his outline being well defined against the sky beyond. The band noiselessly drew up and faced him.

Your money or your life!' said the constable sternly to the still figure.

No, no,' whispered John Pitcher. Tisn't our side ought to say that. That's the doctrine of vagabonds like him, and we be on the side of the law.'

Well, well,' replied the constable impatiently; 'I must say something, mustn't I? and if you had all the weight o' this undertaking upon your mind, perhaps you'd say the wrong thing too!—Prisoner at the bar, surrender, in the name of the Father—the Crown, I mane!'

The man under the tree seemed now to notice them for the first time, and, giving them no opportunity whatever for exhibiting their courage, he strolled slowly towards them. He was, indeed, the little man, the third stranger; but his trepidation had in a great measure gone.

'Well, travellers,' he said, 'did I hear ye speak to me?'

'You did: you've got to come and be our prisoner at once!' said the constable. 'We arrest 'ee on the charge of not biding in Casterbridge jail in a decen proper manner to be hung to-morrow morning Neighbours, do your duty, and seize the culpet!'

On hearing the charge, the man seemed enlightened, and, saying not another word, resigned himself with preternatural civility to the search party, who, with their staves in their hands surrounded him on all sides, and marched him back towards the shepherd's cottage.

It was eleven o'clock by the time they arrived. The light shining from the open door, a sound of men's voices within, proclaimed to them as they approached the house that some new events had arisen in their absence. On entering they discovered the shepherd's living room to be invaded by two officers from Casterbridge jail, and a well-known magistrate who lived at the nearest country-seat intelligence of the escape having become generally circulated.

'Gentlemen,' said the constable, 'I have brought back your man—not without risk and danger; but

very one must do his duty! He is inside this circle
f able-bodied persons, who have lent me useful
id, considering their ignorance of Crown work.
Men, bring forward your prisoner!' And the third
tranger was led to the light.

Who is this?' said one of the officials.

The man,' said the constable.

Certainly not,' said the turnkey; and the first
orroborated his statement.

But how can it be otherwise?' asked the constable.
or why was he so terrified at sight o' the singing
nstrument of the law who sat there?' Here he
elated the strange behaviour of the third stranger
on entering the house during the hangman's song.

Can't understand it,' said the officer coolly. 'All I
now is that it is not the condemned man. He's
quite a different character from this one; a gauntish
ellow, with dark hair and eyes, rather good-
ooking, and with a musical bass voice that if you
heard it once you'd never mistake as long as you
ived.'

Why, souls—'twas the man in the chimney-corner!'

Hey—what?' said the magistrate, coming forward

after inquiring particulars from the shepherd in the background. 'Haven't you got the man after all?'

'Well, sir,' said the constable, 'he's the man we were in search of, that's true; and yet he's not the man we were in search of. For the man we were in search of was not the man we wanted, sir, if you understand my every-day way; for 'twas the man in the chimney-corner!'

'A pretty kettle of fish altogether!' said the magistrate. 'You had better start for the other man at once.'

The prisoner now spoke for the first time. The mention of the man in the chimney-corner seemed to have moved him as nothing else could do. 'Sir,' he said, stepping forward to the magistrate, 'take no more trouble about me. The time is come when I may as well speak. I have done nothing; my crime is that the condemned man is my brother. Early this afternoon I left home at Shottsford to tramp it all the way to Casterbridge jail to bid him farewell. I was benighted, and called here to rest and ask the way. When I opened the door I saw before me the very man, my brother, that I thought to see in the

ondemned cell at Casterbridge. He was in this
chimney-corner; and jammed close to him, so that
he could not have got out if he had tried, was the
executioner who'd come to take his life, singing a
song about it and not knowing that it was his victim
who was close by, joining in to save appearances.
My brother looked a glance of agony at me, and I
knew he meant, "Don't reveal what you see; my life
depends on it." I was so terror-struck that I could
hardly stand, and, not knowing what I did, I turned
and hurried away.'

The narrator's manner and tone had the stamp of
truth, and his story made a great impression on all
round. 'And do you know where your brother is at
the present time?' asked the magistrate.

'I do not. I have never seen him since I closed this
door.'

'I can testify to that, for we've been between ye ever
since,' said the constable.

'Where does he think to fly to?—what is his
occupation?'

'He's a watch-and-clock-maker, sir.'

'A said 'a was a wheelwright—a wicked rogue,' said

the constable.

'The wheels of clocks and watches he meant, n
doubt,' said Shepherd Fennel. 'I thought his hand
were palish for's trade.'

'Well, it appears to me that nothing can be gaine
by retaining this poor man in custody,' said th
magistrate; 'your business lies with the othe
unquestionably.'

And so the little man was released off-hand; but h
looked nothing the less sad on that account, it bein
beyond the power of magistrate or constable to raz
out the written troubles in his brain, for the
concerned another whom he regarded with mor
solicitude than himself. When this was done, an
the man had gone his way, the night was found t
be so far advanced that it was deemed useless t
renew the search before the next morning.

Next day, accordingly, the quest for the cleve
sheep-stealer became general and keen, to al
appearance at least. But the intended punishmen
was cruelly disproportioned to the transgression
and the sympathy of a great many country-folk i
that district was strongly on the side of the fugitive

Moreover, his marvellous coolness and daring in hob-and-nobbing with the hangman, under the unprecedented circumstances of the shepherd's party, won their admiration. So that it may be questioned if all those who ostensibly made themselves so busy in exploring woods and fields and lanes were quite so thorough when it came to the private examination of their own lofts and outhouses. Stories were afloat of a mysterious figure being occasionally seen in some old overgrown trackway or other, remote from turnpike roads; but when a search was instituted in any of these suspected quarters nobody was found. Thus the days and weeks passed without tidings.

In brief, the bass-voiced man of the chimney-corner was never recaptured. Some said that he went across the sea, others that he did not, but buried himself in the depths of a populous city. At any rate, the gentleman in cinder-gray never did his morning's work at Casterbridge, nor met anywhere at all, for business purposes, the genial comrade with whom he had passed an hour of relaxation in the lonely house on the coomb.

The grass has long been green on the graves o
Shepherd Fennel and his frugal wife; the guest:
who made up the christening party have mainly
followed their entertainers to the tomb; the baby ir
whose honour they all had met is a matron in the
sere and yellow leaf. But the arrival of the three
strangers at the shepherd's that night, and the
details connected therewith, is a story as wel
known as ever in the country about Highe:
Crowstairs.

Made in the USA
Monee, IL
14 May 2023

33678176R00052